The Monster That Grew Small

AN EGYPTIAN FOLKTALE

THE MONSTER
THAT GREW SMALL

RETOLD BY JOAN GRANT

ILLUSTRATED BY JILL KARLA SCHWARZ

DESIGNED BY JOHN LYNCH

A JANE LAHR ENTERPRISE

LOTHROP, LEE & SHEPARD BOOKS • NEW YORK

Printed in Hong Kong.

First Edition

1 2 3 4 5 6 7 8 9 10

Library of Congress Cataloging in Publication Data

Grant, Joan Marshall, 1907–
   The monster that grew small.

   Summary: A retelling of an Egyptian folktale in which a
timid boy finds courage by going after a monster that seems
to shrink when confronted.
   [1. Folklore—Egypt] I. Schwarz, Jill Karla, ill. II. Title.
PZ8.1.G736Mo   1987   398.2′1′0962 [E]   86-15302
ISBN 0-688-06808-1
ISBN 0-688-06809-X (lib. bdg.)

Far to the south, beyond the Third Cataract, there was a
small village, where a certain boy lived with his uncle.
The uncle was known as the Brave One, because he was a
hunter and killed such a lot of large animals; and he was
very horrid to his nephew, because he thought the boy
was a coward. He tried to frighten him by telling stories of
the terrible monsters that he said lived in the forest; and
the boy believed what he was told, for was not his uncle
called the Brave One, the Mighty Hunter?

Whenever the boy had to go down to the river, he
thought that crocodiles would eat him; and when he went
into the forest, he thought that the shadows concealed
snakes, and that hairy spiders waited under the leaves to
pounce on him. The place that always felt specially dangerous
was on the path down to the village; and whenever he
had to go along it, he used to run.

One day, when he came to the most frightening

part of this path, he heard a voice crying out from the
shadows of the darkest trees. He put his fingers in his ears
and ran even faster; but he could still hear the voice. His
fear was very loud, but even so he could hear his heart,
and it said to him: "Perhaps the owner of that voice is
much more frightened than you are. You know what it
feels like to be frightened. Don't you think you ought
to help?"

So he took his fingers out of his ears, and clenched his fists to make himself feel braver, and plunged into the deep shade, thrusting his way between thorn trees in the direction of the cries.

He found a Hare, caught by the leg in a tangle of creepers. The Hare said to him, "I was so very frightened; but now you have come, I am not afraid anymore. You must be very brave to have come alone into the forest."

The boy released the Hare and quieted it between his hands, saying, "I am not at all brave. In my village they call me Miobi, the Frightened One. I should never have dared to come here, only I heard you calling."

The Hare said to him, "Why are you frightened? What are you frightened of?"

"I am frightened of the crocodiles who live in the river; and of the snakes, and the spiders, that lie in wait for me whenever I go out. But most of all I am frightened of the Things that rustle in the palm thatch over my bed-place—my uncle says they are only rats and lizards, but *I* know they are far worse than that."

"What you want," said the Hare, "is a house with walls three cubits thick, where you could shut yourself away from all the things you fear."

"I don't think that would do any good," said Miobi. "For if there were no windows, I should be afraid of not being able to breathe; and if there *were* windows, I should always be watching them, waiting for Things to creep in and devour me."

The Hare seemed to have stopped being frightened. Miobi said to it, "Now that you know I am not at all brave, I don't suppose I'll seem much of a protection; but if you feel I'd be better than nothing, I'll carry you home—if you'll tell me where you live."

To Miobi's astonishment, the Hare replied, "I live in the Moon, so you can't come home with me, yet. But I should like to give you something to show how grateful I am for your kindness. What would you like best in the world to have?

"I should like to have Courage. But I suppose that's one of the things that can't be given."

"I can't *give* it to you, but I can tell you where to find it. The road that leads there you will have to follow alone, but when your fears are strongest, look up to the Moon, and I will tell you how to overcome them." Then the Hare told Miobi about the road he must follow.

The next morning, before his uncle was awake, the boy set out on his journey. His only weapon was a dagger that the Hare had given him; it was long and keen, pale as moonlight.

Soon the road came to a wide river; then Miobi was
very frightened, for in it there floated many crocodiles, who
watched him with their evil little eyes. But he remembered
what the Hare had told him, and after looking up to the
Moon, he shouted at them: "If you want to be killed,
come and attack me!"

Then he plunged into the river, his dagger clutched in his hand, and began to swim to the far bank.

Much to the crocodiles' surprise, they found themselves afraid of him. To try to keep up their dignity, they said to one another, "He is too thin to be worth the trouble of eating!" And they shut their eyes and pretended not to notice him. So Miobi crossed the river safely and went on his way.

After a few more days he saw two snakes, each so large that it could have swallowed an ox without getting a pain. Both speaking at the same time, they said loudly, "If you come one step farther, we shall immediately eat you."

Miobi was very frightened, for snakes were one of the things he minded most. He was on the point of running away, but then he looked up to the Moon and knew what the Hare wanted him to do.

"O Large and Intelligent Serpents," he said politely, "a boy so small as myself could do no more than give *one* of you a satisfactory meal; half of me would not be worth the trouble of digesting. Hadn't you better decide between yourselves by whom I am to have the honor of being eaten?"

"Sensible, very. I will eat you myself," said the first serpent.

"No, you won't. He's mine," said the second.

"Nonsense, you had that rich merchant. He was so
busy looking after his gold that he never noticed you, until
you got him by the legs."

"Well, what about the woman who was admiring her
face in a mirror? You said she was the tenderest meal
you'd had for months."

"The merchant was *since* that," said the first serpent
firmly.

"He wasn't."

"He was."

"Wasn't!"

"Was!!"

While the serpents were busy arguing over which of them should eat Miobi, he had slipped past without their noticing, and was already out of sight. So that morning neither of the serpents had even a small breakfast.

Miobi felt so cheerful that he began to whistle. For the first time he found himself enjoying the shapes of trees and the colors of flowers, instead of wondering what dangers they might be concealing.

Soon he came in sight of a village, and even from a distance he could hear the sound of lamentation. As he walked down the single street, no one took any notice of him, for the people were too busy moaning and wailing. The cooking fires were unlit, and goats were bleating because no one had remembered to milk them. Babies were crying because they were hungry, and a small girl was yelling because she had fallen down and cut her knee and her mother wasn't even interested.

Miobi went to the house of the Headman, whom he found sitting cross-legged, with ashes on his head, his

eyes shut, and his fingers in his ears. Miobi had to shout very loud to make him hear.

Then the old man opened one ear and one eye and growled, "What do you want?"

"Nothing," said Miobi politely. "I wanted to ask what *you* wanted. Why is your village so unhappy?"

"You'd be unhappy," said the Headman crossly, "if you were going to be eaten by a Monster."

"Who is going to be eaten? You?"

"Me and everyone else, even the goats; can't you hear them bleating?"

Miobi was too polite to suggest that the goats were bleating only because no one had milked them. So he said to the Headman, "There seem to be quite a lot of people in your village. Couldn't you kill the Monster if you all helped?"

"Impossible!" said the Headman. "Too big, too fierce, too terrible. We are *all* agreed on that."

"What does the Monster look like?" asked Miobi.

"They say it has the head of a crocodile, and the body of a hippopotamus, and a tail like a very fat snake, but it's sure to be even worse. Don't talk about it!" He put his hands over his face and rocked backward and forward, moaning to himself.

"If you will tell me where the Monster lives, I will try to kill it for you," said Miobi, much to his own surprise.

"Perhaps you are wise," said the Headman, "for then you will be eaten first and won't have so long to think about it. The Monster lives in the cave on the top of that mountain. The smoke you can see comes from its fiery breath. You'll be cooked before you are eaten."

Miobi looked up to the Moon and knew what the Hare wanted him to say, so he said it: "I will go up the mountain and challenge the Monster."

Climbing the mountain took him a long time; but when he was halfway up, he could see the Monster quite clearly. Basking at the mouth of its cave, its fiery breath whooshing out of its nostrils, it looked about three times as big as the Royal Barge—which is very big, even for a monster.

Miobi said to himself, "I won't look at it again until I have climbed all the distance between me and the cave; otherwise I might feel too much like running away to be able to go on climbing."

When next he looked at the Monster, he expected it to be much larger than it had seemed from farther away. But instead it looked quite definitely smaller, only a little bigger than one Royal Barge instead of the size of three.

The Monster saw him. It snorted angrily, and the snort flared down the mountainside and scorched Miobi. He ran back rather a long way before he could make himself stop. Now the Monster seemed to have grown larger again; it was *quite* three times as large as the Royal Barge—perhaps four.

Miobi said to himself, "This is very curious indeed. The farther I run away from the Monster, the larger it seems, and the nearer I am to it, the smaller it seems. Perhaps if I was *very* close, it might be a reasonable size for me to kill with my dagger."

So that he would not be blinded by the fiery breath, he shut his eyes; and so that he would not drop his dagger, he clasped it very tightly; and so that he would not have time to start being frightened, he ran as fast as he could up the mountain to the cave.

When he opened his eyes, he couldn't see anything
that needed killing. The cave seemed empty, and he began
to think that he must have run in the wrong direction.
Then he felt something hot touch his right foot. He looked
down, and there was the Monster—and it was as small as
a frog! He picked it up in his hand and scratched its back.
It was no more than comfortably warm to hold, and it
made a small, friendly sound, halfway between a purr and
the simmer of a cooking pot.

Miobi thought, "Poor little Monster! It will feel so
lonely in this enormous cave." Then he thought, "It might
make a nice pet, and its fiery breath would be useful for
lighting my cooking fire." So he carried it carefully down
the mountain, and it curled up in his hand and went to
sleep.

When the villagers saw Miobi, at first they thought
they must be dreaming, for they had been so sure the
Monster would kill him. Then they acclaimed him as a
hero, saying, "Honor to the mighty hunter! He, the
bravest of all! He who has slain the Monster!"

Miobi felt very embarrassed, and as soon as he could
make himself heard above the cheering, he said, "But I
didn't kill it. I brought it home as a pet."

They thought that was only the modesty becoming
to a hero, and before they would believe him he had to
explain how the Monster had only seemed big so long as
he was running away, and that the nearer he got to it the
smaller it grew, until at last, when he was standing beside
it, he could pick it up in his hand.

The people crowded round to see the Monster. It woke up, yawned a small puff of smoke, and began to purr. A little girl asked Miobi, "What is its name?"

"I don't know," said Miobi. "I never asked it."

The Monster itself answered her question. It stopped purring, looked round to make sure everyone was listening, and then said:

"I have many names. Some call me Famine, and some Pestilence; but the most pitiable of humans give me their own names." It yawned again, and then added, "But most people call me What-Might-Happen."